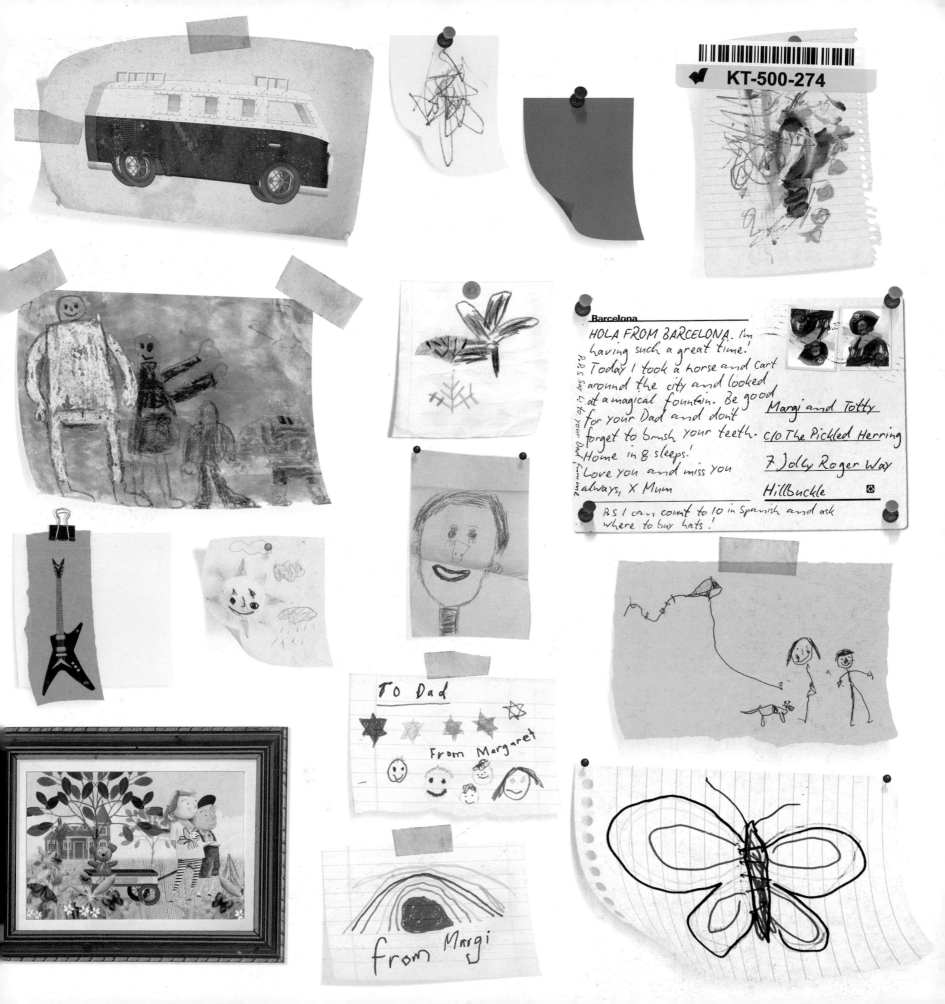

Barcelona

HOLA FROM BARCELONA. I'm
having such a great time!
Today I took a horse and cart
around the city and looked
at a magical fountain. Be good
for your Dad and don't
forget to brush your teeth.
Home in 8 sleeps!
Love you and miss you
always, X Mum

P.P.S Say hi to your Dad from me

Margi and Totty
c/o The Pickled Herring

7 Jolly Roger Way

Hillbuckle

P.S I can count to 10 in Spanish and ask
where to buy hats!

TO Dad

From Margaret

from Margi

For my dad Robin, a
collector of bits and
bobs, and my amazing
mum Rose.
K.L

For Mum
- who can't throw
anything away!
B.G

First published in 2008 by Hodder Children's Books
First published in paperback in 2009

Text copyright © Kiri Lightfoot 2008
Illustrations copyright © Ben Galbraith 2008

Hodder Children's Books
338 Euston Road
London NW1 3BH

Hodder Children's Books Australia
Level 17/207 Kent Street
Sydney NSW 2000

The right of Kiri Lightfoot to be identified as the author and Ben Galbraith to be
identified as the illustrator of this Work has been asserted by them in accordance
with the Copyright, Designs and Patents Act 1988.

A catalogue record of this book is available from
the British Library.

ISBN: 978 0 340 95613 7

10 9 8 7 6 5 4 3 2 1

Printed in China
Colour Reproduction by Dot Gradations Ltd, UK

Hodder Children's Books is a division of
Hachette Children's Books

An Hachette UK Company
www.hachette.co.uk

Hodder
Children's
Books

EVERY
SECOND
FRIDAY

Written by Kiri Lightfoot · Illustrated by Ben Galbraith

Our dad is a collector of bits and bobs.

Every second Friday my brother and I pack our bags and go and stay at his house.

ME:
Margaret Madeleine
(nickname Margi)
AGE 6 ½

MY BROTHER:
Thomas Theodore
(nickname Totty)
AGE 4 ¾

EETLE

I pack my

toothbrush

pyjamas

books

teddy

and I always pack an extra set of clothes.

Because when we stay at Dad's
house we always get –

magnificently
muddy,
worryingly wet
and
mind-blowingly
messy.

Every second Friday after our
mum has waved us goodbye,

we make our way into Dad's house.

This isn't an easy task.

We always have to push hard against the door.

It's tricky to open when there's
so much stuff.

Once we've squeezed
our way inside
we call out to
Dad and then he'll
pop up behind a piano,
a bookshelf or a car engine.
Dad's house is such a mess
that it's sometimes
hard to find the people.

Our Dad just loves collecting
STUFF - from books and bicycles
to clocks and clarinets, from
pictures and pans to ties and tea towels.
There's nothing he doesn't collect.

We love searching for treasures with Dad. And we especially love exploring Dad's house, admiring the things he's found.

We look through all Dad's hats and ties and shirts and shoes.

We always find something extremely silly for Dad to wear.

Heave-ho me hearties!

Then we rummage through
plates and cups and teapots and
bowls and knives and forks
and we set our table.

THE PICKLED
HERRING

Then we hunt through
toys and puppets and dolls
and teddies and find
our guests.

Then
we
have
a
PARTY !

When we've finished our cups of tea
we search through Dad's
old records and tapes and
we dance to jingles and waltzes
and rock and roll and Beethoven.

When we're tired from all
the looking, rummaging, hunting,
searching and dancing we climb
over guitars and paintings and
letter boxes to find our beds.

Then our Dad, a collector of
bits and bobs, tucks us up in bed and
tells us how much fun he's had and
how special we are to him.

But we already knew that of course ...

BEST HATS

Because Dad's favourite things to collect are photos of us, and all the drawings we've done for him.

He puts them up all over the walls and on the fridge and next to his bed.

And that's
how we know that
our Dad's house is
our house too!

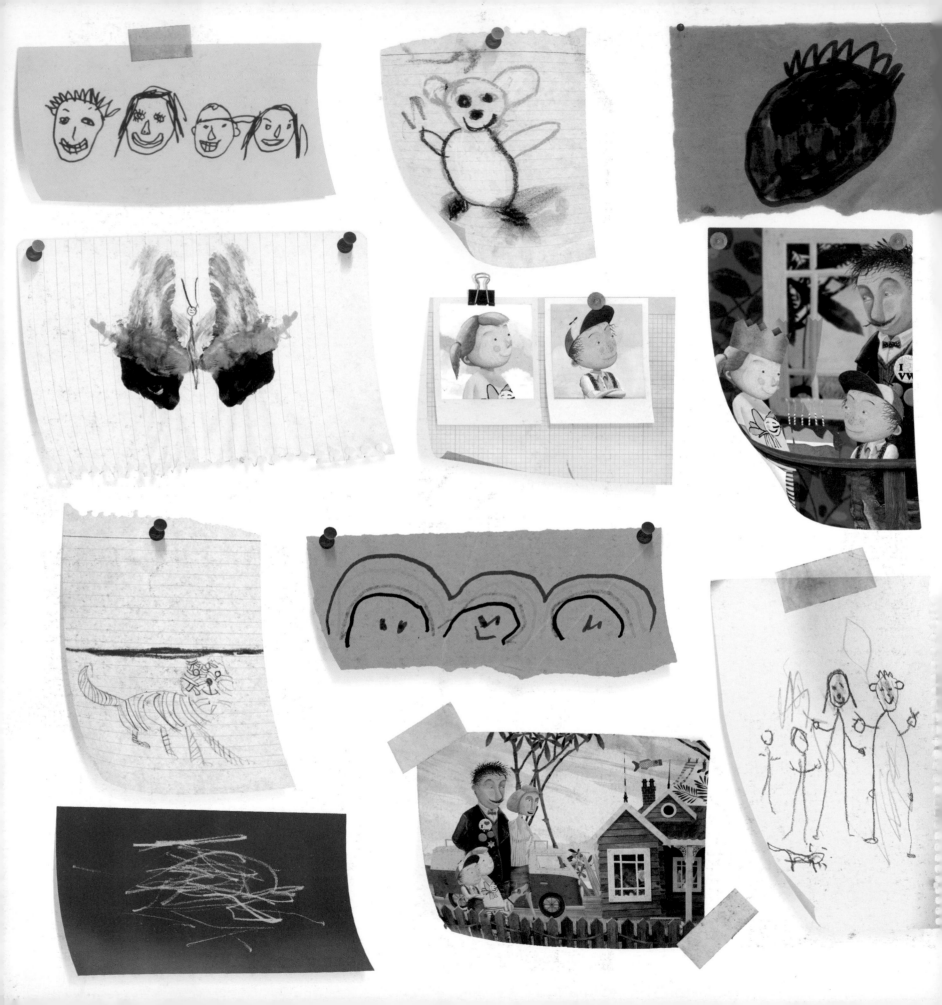

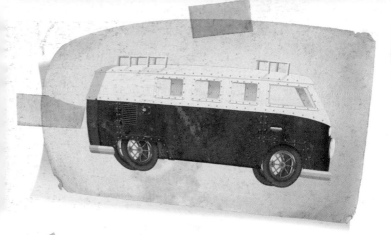

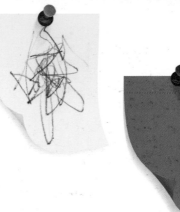

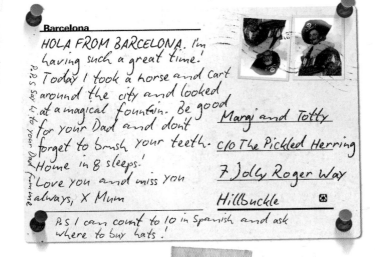

To Dad

From Margaret

from Margi

Other great Hodder picture books perfect to share with children:

978 0 340 89342 5

978 0 340 94508 7

978 0 340 94482 0

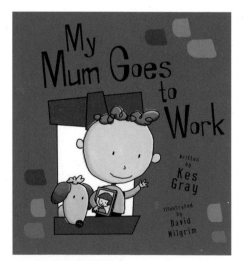

978 0 340 88369 3

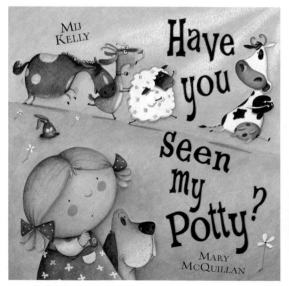

978 0 340 91153 2

Hodder Children's Books

A division of Hachette Children's Books